leapfrog

Rhyme
Time

Squeaky
Clean

First published in 2006 by
Franklin Watts
338 Euston Road
London
NW1 3BH

Franklin Watts Australia
Hachette Children's Books
Level 17/207 Kent Street
Sydney
NSW 2000

Text © Jane Clarke 2006
Illustration © Anni Axworthy 2006

A CIP catalogue record for this book is available
from the British Library.

ISBN 0 7496 6588 2 (hbk)
ISBN 0 7496 6805 9 (pbk)

Series Editor: Jackie Hamley
Series Advisor: Dr Barrie Wade
Series Designer: Peter Scoulding

Printed in China

Squeaky
Clean

by Jane Clarke

Illustrated by Anni Axworthy

W

FRANKLIN WATTS

LONDON•SYDNEY

Little Ellie has a scheme

to keep the whole zoo
squeaky clean.

Watch out animals,
big and small!

Here she comes to
squirt you all!

7

When Ellie turns her
trunk to spray,

three tiny mice are

washed away.

Ellie needs an extra squirt
to blast off Hippo's
crust of dirt.

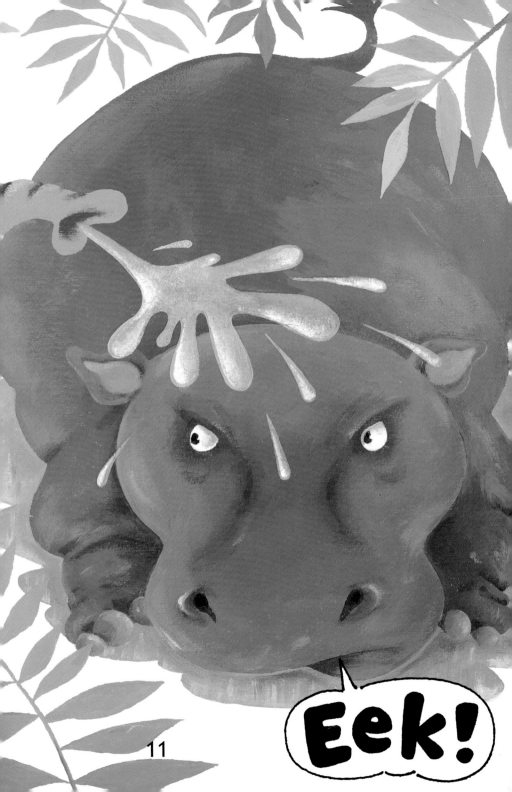

11

She has to shoot
a water jet

to reach the top
of Giraffe's neck.

Even Skunk smells
like a flower

after Ellie's power shower.

She's not afraid,
she has no fears
of Crocodile's teeth ...

16

... or Tiger's ears.

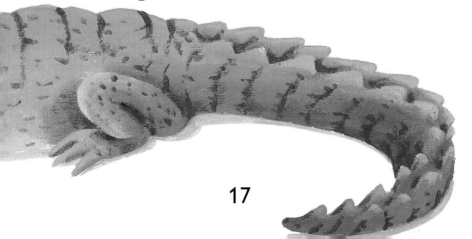

Anaconda's looking grimy,

but Ellie makes him bright
and shiny.

She washes apes
and kangaroos

with foamy soap suds
and shampoos.

Now she's scrubbing
Leopard's belly.

But Leopard's never
spotless, Ellie!

And zebras are meant
to be striped,

no matter how hard
they are wiped!

When animals want
to be smelly,
you just can't keep
them clean ...

... poor Ellie.

Now Ellie has a
scheme that's new,

and they're all
happy at the zoo.

Watch out visitors, big and small!

30

Drop litter and she'll
squirt you all!

Leapfrog has been specially designed to fit the requirements of the National Literacy Strategy. It offers real books for beginning readers by top authors and illustrators. There are 43 Leapfrog stories to choose from:

The Bossy Cockerel
ISBN 0 7496 3828 1

Bill's Baggy Trousers
ISBN 0 7496 3829 X

Mr Spotty's Potty
ISBN 0 7496 3831 1

Little Joe's Big Race
ISBN 0 7496 3832 X

The Little Star
ISBN 0 7496 3833 8

The Cheeky Monkey
ISBN 0 7496 3830 3

Selfish Sophie
ISBN 0 7496 4385 4

Recycled!
ISBN 0 7496 4388 9

Felix on the Move
ISBN 0 7496 4387 0

Pippa and Poppa
ISBN 0 7496 4386 2

Jack's Party
ISBN 0 7496 4389 7

The Best Snowman
ISBN 0 7496 4390 0

Eight Enormous Elephants
ISBN 0 7496 4634 9

Mary and the Fairy
ISBN 0 7496 4633 0

The Crying Princess
ISBN 0 7496 4632 2

Jasper and Jess
ISBN 0 7496 4081 2

The Lazy Scarecrow
ISBN 0 7496 4082 0

The Naughty Puppy
ISBN 0 7496 4383 8

Freddie's Fears
ISBN 0 7496 4382 X

Cinderella
ISBN 0 7496 4228 9

The Three Little Pigs
ISBN 0 7496 4227 0

Jack and the Beanstalk
ISBN 0 7496 4229 7

The Three Billy Goats Gruff
ISBN 0 7496 4226 2

Goldilocks and the Three Bears
ISBN 0 7496 4225 4

Little Red Riding Hood
ISBN 0 7496 4224 6

Rapunzel
ISBN 0 7496 6159 3

Snow White
ISBN 0 7496 6161 5

The Emperor's New Clothes
ISBN 0 7496 6163 1

The Pied Piper of Hamelin
ISBN 0 7496 6164 X

Hansel and Gretel
ISBN 0 7496 6162 3

The Sleeping Beauty
ISBN 0 7496 6160 7

Rumpelstiltskin
ISBN 0 7496 6153 4*
ISBN 0 7496 6165 8

The Ugly Duckling
ISBN 0 7496 6154 2*
ISBN 0 7496 6166 6

Puss in Boots
ISBN 0 7496 6155 0*
ISBN 0 7496 6167 4

The Frog Prince
ISBN 0 7496 6156 9*
ISBN 0 7496 6168 2

The Princess and the Pea
ISBN 0 7496 6157 7*
ISBN 0 7496 6169 0

Dick Whittington
ISBN 0 7496 6158 5*
ISBN 0 7496 6170 4

Squeaky Clean
ISBN 0 7496 6588 2*
ISBN 0 7496 6805 9

Craig's Crocodile
ISBN 0 7496 6589 0*
ISBN 0 7496 6806 7

Felicity Floss: Tooth Fairy
ISBN 0 7496 6590 4*
ISBN 0 7496 6807 5

Captain Cool
ISBN 0 7496 6591 2*
ISBN 0 7496 6808 3

Monster Cake
ISBN 0 7496 6592 0*
ISBN 0 7496 6809 1

The Super Trolley Ride
ISBN 0 7496 6593 9*
ISBN 0 7496 6810 5